致敬译界巨匠许渊冲先生

许渊冲译
白居易诗选
SELECTED POEMS OF BAI JUYI

| 编 | 译 |

中国出版集团
中译出版社

目录

Contents

	译序
	Translator's Preface
002	赋得古原草送别
	Grass on the Ancient Plain—Farewell to a Friend
004	望月有感
	By the Light of the Moon
006	邯郸冬至夜思家
	Thinking of Home on Winter Solstice Night at Handan
008	长恨歌
	The Everlasting Regret
022	赠卖松者
	For the Seller of Dwarf Pines
024	上阳白发人
	The White-haired Palace Maid
030	卖炭翁
	The Old Charcoal Seller
034	同李十一醉忆元九
	Thinking of Yuan Zhen While Drinking with Li Eleventh
036	望驿台
	For Roaming Yuan Zhen
038	江楼月
	The Moon over the Riverside Tower
040	买花
	Buying Flowers
044	惜牡丹花
	The Last Look at the Peonies at Night
046	村夜
	One Night in the Village

048	欲与元八卜邻，先有是赠	
	On Becoming Neighbor of Yuan Eighth	
050	燕子楼（三首其一）	
	The Pavilion of Swallows (I)	
052	燕子楼（三首其二）	
	The Pavilion of Swallows (II)	
054	燕子楼（三首其三）	
	The Pavilion of Swallows (III)	
056	花非花	
	A Flower in the Haze	
058	初贬官过望秦岭	
	Passing by the Head-turning Peak in Banishment	
060	蓝桥驿见元九诗	
	Reading Yuan Zhen's Poem at Blue Bridge Post	
062	舟中读元九诗	
	Reading Yuan Zhen's Poems on a Boat	
064	放言	
	Written at Random	
066	琵琶行	
	Song of a Pipa Player	
078	南浦别	
	Farewell by Southern Riverside	
080	大林寺桃花	
	Peach Blossoms in the Temple of Great Forest	
082	遗爱寺	
	Temple of Dear Memories	
084	问刘十九	
	An Invitation	

086	夜雪	Snowing at Night
088	钟陵饯送	Farewell Feast at Zhongling
090	李白墓	Li Bai's Grave
092	后宫词	The Deserted
094	夜筝	Lute Playing at Night
096	勤政楼西老柳	The Old Willow Tree West of the Administrative Hall
098	暮江吟	Sunset and Moonrise on the River
100	寒闺怨	A Wife's Grief in Autumn
102	钱塘湖春行	On Lake Qiantang in Spring
104	春题湖上	The Lake in Spring
106	西湖晚归回望孤山寺赠诸客	Looking Back at the Lonely Hill on My Way across West Lake
108	杭州春望	Spring View in Hangzhou
110	别州民	Farewell to the People of Hangzhou
112	白云泉	White Cloud Fountain

114 秋雨夜眠
Sleeping on a Rainy Autumn Night

116 与梦得沽酒闲饮且约后期
Drinking Together with Liu Yuxi

118 览卢子蒙侍御旧诗，多与微之唱和，感今伤昔，
因赠子蒙，题于卷后
On Reading Lu Zimeng's Old Poems Written in the Same Rhyme Schemes as Yuan Zhen's Poems

120 红鹦鹉
The Red Cockatoo

122 昼卧
Depression

124 病中
Illness

126 杨柳枝词
Song of Willow Branch

128 忆江南
Fair South Recalled

130 长相思
Everlasting Longing

译序

白居易（772—846）是我国唐代伟大的现实主义诗人，字乐天，号香山居士，祖籍太原，生于河南新郑，幼年时代在中原一带度过。公元787年，他16岁时初到京城长安，带着诗集去见当时的名士顾况。顾况看了他的名字就说："米价方贵，居亦弗易。"当顾况翻开诗集，读到《赋得古原草送别》中的"野火烧不尽，春风吹又生"时，不禁赞道："能写出这样的诗句，居亦易矣！"于是白居易声名大振。

公元799年，白居易在河南经历了叛军之乱，兄弟离散，写下了《自河南经乱》一诗，说出了战乱给人民带来的苦难，以及兄弟间的关怀之情。公元800年，他29岁时进士及第。公元806年，他在今天的陕西周至县任县尉，写下了著名的《长恨歌》。诗中对唐明皇的好色误国有所讽喻，但对他和杨贵妃的爱情故事，则表示了深切的同情。诗的艺术性很强，作者运用了浪漫主义手法，写来感情丰富，词彩绚丽，形象动人，具有强烈的感染力，是千百年来人们传诵的名篇。关于爱情的诗歌，他还写了《燕子楼》《花非花》等小诗。

公元808年，白居易任左拾遗（一种谏议朝政得失的官吏）时，有三个考生因为抨击时政，触犯了宰相等保守派，牵连了许多人被贬官。白居易上书请求改变这一决定，同时写了《赠卖松者》一诗，通过描写松树的无地栽种来影射人才的不容于世。他后来写的《红鹦鹉》《杨柳枝词》等，也属于这一类讽喻诗。

公元809年，白居易又写了50首《新乐府》，全面深入地揭露了唐代中期的黑暗面，触及许多社会问题。本书选了两首：一首是《上阳白发人》，写一个宫女被幽禁的典型事例，控诉了封建帝王占有三宫六院的罪恶制度，同时对后宫的怨女表示了深刻的同情；另一首是《卖炭翁》，描写皇室在长安市上公开掠夺民间财物，作者用很少的笔墨把人物写活，有典型的社会意义，表现了强烈的人道主义精神。

公元810年前后，白居易还写了10首《秦中吟》，序言中说："予在长安，闻见之间，有足悲者，因直歌其事。"作者对当时不合理的社会现象，进行了激烈的抨击。这里选了一首《买花》，揭露了达官贵人的挥霍奢靡，批评了贵人"一丛深色花，十户中人赋"的不平现象。

公元815年，白居易被贬为江州司马，同时，他的好友元稹也再度被贬。本书选了几首表现他们之间深厚友情的诗，如《蓝桥驿见元九诗》《舟中读元九诗》等。这些诗出语虽然平淡，关切之情却很深沉。

白居易在江州最著名的作品自然是《琵琶行》。这首诗通过一个歌女的遭遇，写出了社会上的幸与不幸。作者以强烈的感情色彩和高超的艺术手法，描述了歌女弹琵琶的精湛技艺和她的苦难身世，塑造了一个典型的艺术形象。他还再进一步，倾诉了自己屈遭贬谪，有志难申的满腔义愤。歌女和诗人都有非凡的才华，却又同样遭到朝廷和社会的弃置。关于这方面的天涯沦落人，作者还在《李白墓》等诗中，表露了他的深刻同情。

　　在江州时,白居易在庐山香炉峰下修建了一座草堂,常去附近的花径、山下的遗爱寺、山上的大林寺等地游玩,写下了《大林寺桃花》《遗爱寺》等小诗,前者平中见奇,后者景中见情。自然,他大量的写景诗还是公元822—824年任杭州刺史时的作品。他赴杭州途中写的《暮江吟》,写出了日落和月出时的迷人景色。《钱塘湖春行》通过初春的云雨、湖水、莺燕、花草等几个有典型意义的细节特征,把西湖胜景展现在人们面前,使人明白他为什么"未能抛得杭州去,一半勾留是此湖"。他离开杭州时写了一首《别州民》,充分显示了他对人民的关怀之情。公元825年他任苏州刺史,写了一首《白云泉》,反映了他要退隐云水之间、随遇而安的思想。这种思想在《昼卧》《病中》等诗中也有所流露。

　　白居易的诗词创作大致可分前后两个时期。在去江州之前,他的政治热情很高,关心国家大事和人民生活,写了大量的进步诗歌。被贬江州之后,消极思想渐占上风,不再热衷政治。其作品通俗易懂,在当时和后世,都有巨大的影响。

Translator's Preface

On seventh day of seventh moon when none was near,
At midnight in Long Life Hall he whispered in her ear:
"On high, we'd be two birds flying wing to wing;
On earth, two trees with branches twined from spring to spring."

(*The Everlasting Regret*)

Such is the story of Emperor Xuan Zong of the Tang Dynasty and his favorite Lady Yang as told by Bai Juyi in his favorite poem which ended in the army's revolt and in her tragical death was considered as a turning point of the Tang Dynasty. Since olden days the decline and fall of dynasties hinged more or less on the imperial indulgence in wine, woman, and song. So this poem of Bai's was considered as important as an epic or a record of history.

In ancient epics, three methods of versification were used, that is, narration, comparison, and association. In the poem cited above, we find narration in the first couplet, comparison in the second and association in the third. For the poet compares the lovers to birds and trees and the boundless sky and endless earth are associated with the everlasting regret. Of these three methods, narration is often used. It may be used to describe a man, for example, in *The Old Charcoal Seller*:

What does the old man fare?
He cuts the wood in southern hill and fires his ware.
His face is grimed with smoke and streaked with ash and dust,
His temples grizzled and his fingers all turned black.
The money earned by selling charcoal is not just
Enough for food his mouth and clothing for his back.

It may describe such a scene as sunset or moonrise on the river:

The departing sunbeams pave a way on the river;
Half of its waves turn red and the other half shiver.
How I love the third night of the ninth moon aglow!
The dewdrops look like pearls, the crescent like a bow.

The narration is more elaborate, and in the last line we have the comparion of dewdrops to pearls and of the new moon to a bow. Bai's best-known comparisons is found in the *Song of a Pipa Player*:

The thick strings loudly thrummed like the pattering rain;

V

> *The fine strings softly tinkled in a murmuring strain.*
> *When mingling loud and soft notes were together played,*
> *You heard large and small pearls cascade on plate of jade.*

Sometimes it is not easy to distinguish comparison from association. For example, in *The Red Cockatoo*:

> *But it is shut up in a cage with bar on bar*
> *Just as the learned or eloquent scholars are.*

On seeing a cockatoo shut up in a cage, the poet thinks of an unemployed scholar like the caged bird. It is association more than comparison. Another example in *A Flower in the Haze*:

> *In bloom, she's not a flower;*
> *Hazy, she's not a haze.*
> *She comes at midnight hour;*
> *She goes with starry rays.*
> *She comes like vernal dreams that cannot stay;*
> *She goes like morning clouds that melt away.*

On the one hand, the poet seems to compare the heroine to a flower or a haze, to a dream or a cloud, and on the other hand, the dream that cannot stay and the cloud that will melt are symbols of the heroine, they are not comparison but symbolism. Comparison is to find the resemblance in similar things, while a symbolist may find resemblance in dissimilar things. For another example, we may read Bai's *White Cloud Fountain*:

Behold the White Cloud Fountain on the Sky-blue Mountain.
White clouds enjoy free pleasure; water enjoy leisure.
Why should the torrent dash down from the mountain high
And overflow the human world with waves far and nigh?

Clouds and water are dissimilar things, but the poet finds their love of freedom in common. In reality, neither clouds nor water enjoy free pleasure as the poet, so they become the symbols of the poet. So this verse is not comparative but symbolic, though it is written in words simple and clear.

Bai's verse is so simple and clear that even uneducated old women could understand it. It is true, but some critic goes as far as saying that Bai's poems seem to have been written not for but by an old woman. For example, in *An Invitation* he says:

At dusk it threatens snow.
Won't you come for a cup?

It seems true, so far as his narration is concerned. But it would be different when we come to comparison and association. Do we not find the following verse in his *The Everlasting Regret* as romantic as Li Bai:

The moon viewed from his tent sheds a soul-searing light;
The bells heard in night rain made a heart-rending sound.

Is not the description of the *The Old Charcoal Seller* as realistic as Du Fu's *The Pressgang at Stone Moat Village*? Is not *A Flower in the Haze* as symbolic as Li Shangyin's *To One Unnamed Lover*? Bai Juyi is as popular as Li Bai is romantic, as Du Fu is realistic and as Li Shangyin is symbolic.

许渊冲译白居易诗选

赋得①古原草送别

① 赋得：借古人诗句或成语命题作诗，即在指定、限定的题目上加"赋得"二字。古人学习作诗、文人聚会分题作诗或科举考试时命题作诗的一种方式，被称为"赋得体"。

离离②原上草，
一岁一枯荣。
野火烧不尽，
春风吹又生。
远芳③侵④古道，
晴翠接荒城。
又送王孙⑤去，
萋萋⑥满别情。

② 离离：形容草茂盛的样子。

③ 芳：野草浓郁的香气。

④ 侵：侵占，长满。

⑤ 王孙：本指贵族后代，此处指作者的友人。

⑥ 萋萋：形容草木繁盛的样子。

这首诗是公元787年白居易16岁应考时的作品。第一联起写草，说原上草多么茂盛，每年枯萎了还会新生。第二联承，"野火烧"是说草"枯"，"吹又生"是说草"荣"。第三联转为写古原：古道荒城，因为远近都长满了芳草，清香扑鼻；一片青翠，沐浴在阳光中，欣欣向荣。第四联写送别：看见萋萋芳草，更增添了送别的愁思，仿佛每一片草叶都饱含着别情似的。于是古原草和送别就合而为一了。

Grass on the Ancient Plain
— Farewell to a Friend

Wild grasses spread o'er ancient plain;

With spring and fall they come and go.

Fire tries to burn them up in vain;

They rise again when spring winds blow.

Their fragrance overruns the way;

Their green invades the ruined town.

To see my friend going away;

My sorrow grows like grass o'ergrown.

望月有感

时难年荒①世业②空,
弟兄羁旅各西东。
田园寥落干戈③后,
骨肉流离道路中。
吊影④分为千里雁⑤,
辞根⑥散作九秋蓬⑦。
共看明月应垂泪,
一夜乡心五处同。

① 时难年荒:指遭受战乱和灾荒。
② 世业:祖传的产业。唐代初实行"授田制",死后子孙可继承"世业田"。
③ 干戈:干和戈为古代两种兵器,此处代指战争。
④ 吊影:一个人孤单的身影。
⑤ 千里雁:比喻兄弟相隔千里,宛如离群的孤雁。
⑥ 辞根:草木离开根部,比喻背井离乡。
⑦ 九秋蓬:深秋随风飘荡的蓬草,用来比喻游子在异乡漂泊。九秋:即秋天。

公元799年,河南兵荒马乱,白居易兄弟离散,他写了这一首抒怀诗。在这灾难深重的年代,白家祖业荡然一空,同胞骨肉天各一方。回首故乡田园,在战乱中一片寥落凄清;兄弟姊妹奔波在异乡道路上,犹如纷飞千里的孤雁,只能吊影自怜;或像深秋时断根的蓬草,随着萧瑟

By the Light of the Moon

Hard times with famine spread ruins in our home town;

My brothers go their way east or west, up and down.

Battles have left the fields and gardens desolate;

By roadside wander families were separate.

Like far-off wild geese over lonely shadows we weep,

As scattered rootless tumbleweed in autumn deep.

We should shed yearning tears to view the moon apart;

Though in five places, we have the same homesick heart.

的西风飘转不定。夜深人静，诗人看到明月，不禁想起分散在各地的亲人。如果他们也在望月，会不会和自己一样流下思乡之泪呢？这首诗用白描的手法、平易的语言，写出了人所共有的情感。奇语易，常语难，这首七律却可以说是"用常得奇"的佳作。

邯郸冬至夜思家

邯郸①驿②里逢冬至,
抱膝灯前影伴身③。
想得家中夜深坐,
还应说着远行人④。

① 邯(hán)郸(dān):地名,今河北省邯郸市。
② 驿:驿站,古代传送公文、转运货物或官员出差途中休息的地方。
③ 影伴身:影子与自己相伴,形容孤独。
④ 远行人:离家在外的人,此处指作者自己。

在唐代,冬至是个重要的节日。朝廷放假,民间互赠饮食,穿新衣,贺节,一切都和元旦相似。公元804年的这一天,诗人却在客店里度过,只有抱膝枯坐的影子和他作伴,孤寂之感、思家之情,油然而生。自己思家直到深夜,料想家人也没有睡,也在想着说着远行在外的自己。这首诗是写"每逢佳节倍思亲",是一首感情真挚动人的作品。

Thinking of Home on Winter Solstice Night at Handan

At roadside inn I pass the Winter Solstice Day,
Clasping my knees, my shadow is my company,
I think, till dead of night my family would stay,
And talk about the poor lonely wayfaring me.

长恨歌

许渊冲译白居易诗选

汉皇①重色思倾国②,
御宇③多年求不得。
杨家有女初长成,
养在深闺人未识。
天生丽质难自弃,
一朝选在君王侧。
回眸一笑百媚生,
六宫粉黛④无颜色。
春寒赐浴华清池⑤,
温泉水滑洗凝脂⑥。
侍儿扶起娇无力,
始是新承恩泽⑦时。
云鬓⑧花颜金步摇⑨,
芙蓉帐⑩暖度春宵。

① 汉皇:原指汉武帝刘彻,此处借指唐玄宗李隆基。
② 倾国:绝色女子。"倾国倾城"常用来形容或指代美女。
③ 御宇:驾御宇内,即统治天下。

④ 六宫粉黛:指宫中所有的嫔妃;粉黛:本为化妆用品,粉以涂脸,黛以描眉,此处代指女性。
⑤ 华清池:即华清池温泉,今西安市骊山脚下。唐贞观十八年(644年)建汤泉宫,后改名为华清宫。唐玄宗每年冬、春季节都到此居住。
⑥ 凝脂:形容皮肤白嫩细腻,宛如凝固的脂肪。
⑦ 承恩泽:得到君王的宠幸。
⑧ 云鬓(bìn):形容女子浓厚而柔美的鬓发。
⑨ 金步摇:一种金首饰,插于发髻,走路时摇曳生姿。
⑩ 芙蓉帐:绣着莲花的帐子,形容帐之精美。

《长恨歌》是白居易传诵千古的名作,集叙事、写景、抒情于一体,借着历史的影子,根据民间的传说,写出了唐玄宗和杨贵妃在安史之乱

The Everlasting Regret

The beauty-loving monarch longed year after year
To find a beautiful lady without a peer.
A maiden of the Yangs to womanhood just grown,
In inner chambers bred, to the world was unknown.
Endowed with natural beauty too hard to hide,
She was chosen one day to be the monarch's bride.
Turning her head, she smiled so sweet and full of grace
That she outshone in six palaces the fairest face.
She bathed in glassy water of Warm-fountain Pool,
Which laved and smoothed her creamy skin when spring was cool.
Without her maids' support, she was too tired to move,
And this was when she first received the monarch's love.
Flower-like face and cloud-like hair, golden-headdressed,
In lotus-adorned curtain she spent the night blessed.

中的爱情悲剧。诗人把缠绵悱恻之情，写得令人回肠荡气，于是《长恨歌》就成了千古绝唱。

春宵苦短日高起,
从此君王不早朝。
承欢侍宴无闲暇,
春从春游夜专夜。
后宫佳丽三千人,
三千宠爱在一身。
金屋①妆成娇侍夜,
玉楼宴罢醉和春。
姊妹弟兄皆列土②,
可怜③光彩生门户。
遂令天下父母心,
不重生男重生女。
骊宫高处入青云,
仙乐风飘处处闻。
缓歌慢舞凝丝竹④,
尽日君王看不足。
渔阳⑤鼙鼓⑥动地来,
惊破霓裳羽衣曲⑦。

① 金屋：典故出自《汉武故事》，汉武帝刘彻曾言："若得阿娇作妇，当作金屋贮之"，用以指女子受宠。

② 列土：分封土地。

③ 可怜：可爱，令人羡慕。

④ 凝丝竹：弦乐器和管乐器奏出舒缓的旋律。

⑤ 渔阳：郡名，今北京市平谷区和天津市蓟县等地。

⑥ 鼙(pí)鼓：古时军中使用的战鼓，此处借指战争。

⑦ 霓(ní)裳羽衣曲：唐代宫廷舞曲，据传为唐玄宗根据古曲改编，最初用于在太清宫祭献老子时演奏。

She slept till the sun rose high for the blessed night was short,
From then on the monarch held no longer morning court.
In revels as in feasts she shared her lord's delight,
His companion on trips and his mistress at night.
In inner palace dwelt three thousand ladies fair;
On her alone was lavished royal love and care.
Her beauty served the night when dressed up in Golden Bower;
She was drunk with wine and spring at banquet in Jade Tower.
Her sisters and brothers all received rank and fief,
And honors showered on her household, to the grief
Of fathers and mothers who would rather give birth
To a fair maiden than to any son on earth.
The lofty palace towered high into the cloud;
With divine music borne on the breeze the air was loud.
Seeing slow dance and hearing fluted or stringed song,
The emperor was never tired the whole day long.
But rebels beat their war drums, making the earth quake
And *Song of Rainbow Skirt and Coat of Feathers* break.

九重城阙①烟尘生,
千乘万骑西南行。
翠华②摇摇行复止,
西出都门百余里。
六军不发无奈何,
宛转③蛾眉④马前死。
花钿⑤委地⑥无人收,
翠翘金雀玉搔头⑦。
君王掩面救不得,
回看血泪相和流。
黄埃散漫风萧索,
云栈⑧萦纡⑨登剑阁⑩。
峨嵋山下少人行,
旌旗无光日色薄。
蜀江水碧蜀山青,
圣主朝朝暮暮情。
行宫见月伤心色,
夜雨闻铃⑪断肠声。

① 九重城阙:九重门的宫殿,此处代指皇宫。

② 翠华:用翠鸟羽毛装饰而成的旗帜,皇帝仪仗队用。

③ 宛转:形容美人临死之前哀怨、楚楚可怜的样子。

④ 蛾眉:古代美女的代称,此处指杨贵妃。

⑤ 花钿(diàn):用金翠珠宝等制成的花形首饰。

⑥ 委地:丢弃在地上。

⑦ 翠翘金雀玉搔头:均为首饰,翠翘,形如翡翠鸟尾;金雀,金雀钗,钗形似朱雀(凤);玉搔头,玉簪。

⑧ 云栈:高入云霄的栈道。

⑨ 萦(yíng)纡(yū):迂回盘绕。

⑩ 剑阁:即剑门关,是由秦入蜀的要道。该地群山如剑,峭壁中断处,两山对峙如门。

⑪ 夜雨闻铃:《明皇杂录·补遗》中记载"明皇既幸蜀,西南行,初入斜谷,属霖雨涉旬,于栈道雨中闻铃,音与山相应。上既悼念贵妃,采其声为《雨霖铃曲》,以寄恨焉。"此处暗指此事。这也是《雨霖铃》词牌名的来历。

A cloud of dust was raised o'er city walls nine-fold;
Thousands of chariots and horsemen southwestward rolled.
Imperial flags moved slowly now and halted then,
And thirty miles from Western Gate they stopped again.
Six armies — what could be done — would not march with speed,
Unless fair Lady Yang be killed before the steed.
None would pick up her hairpin fallen on the ground,
Nor golden bird nor comb with which her head was crowned.
The monarch could not save her and hid his face in fear;
Turning his head, he saw her blood mix with his tear.
The yellow dust widespread, the wind blew desolate;
A serpentine plank path led to cloud-capped Sword Gate.
Below the Eyebrow Mountains wayfarers were few;
In fading sunlight royal standards lost their hue.
On Western water blue and Western mountains green,
The monarch's heart was daily gnawed by sorrow keen.
The moon viewed from his tent shed a soul-searing light;
The bells heard in night rain made a heart-rending sound.

天旋地转^①回龙驭,
到此踌躇不能去。
马嵬坡下泥土中,
不见玉颜空死处。
君臣相顾尽沾衣,
东望都门信马^②归。
归来池苑皆依旧,
太液^③芙蓉未央^④柳。
芙蓉如面柳如眉,
对此如何不泪垂!
春风桃李花开日,
秋雨梧桐叶落时。
西宫南内多秋草,
落叶满阶红不扫。
梨园弟子^⑤白发新,
椒房^⑥阿监^⑦青娥^⑧老。
夕殿萤飞思悄然,
孤灯挑尽^⑨未成眠。

① 天旋地转:此处指时局好转。

② 信马:意为无心鞭马,任马前进。

③ 太液:长安大明宫北的太液池。

④ 未央:长安皇宫中的未央宫。

⑤ 梨园弟子:指唐玄宗当年训练的乐工舞女。

⑥ 椒房:后妃居住之所,因以花椒和泥抹墙,故称椒房。

⑦ 阿监:宫中的侍从女官。

⑧ 青娥:年轻的宫女。

⑨ 孤灯挑尽:古时用油灯照明,为使灯火保持明亮,需要不时把浸在油中的灯草挑一下。挑尽,说明夜已深。旧时唐宫中夜间燃烛而非油灯,此处也暗示唐玄宗晚年生活的凄苦。

Suddenly turned the tide. Returning from his flight,
The monarch could not tear himself away from the ground.
Where 'mid the clods beneath the Slope he couldn't forget
The fair-faced Lady Yang who was unfairly slain.
He looked at his courtiers, with tears his robe was wet;
They rode east to the capital but with loose rein.
Come back; he found her pond and garden in old place,
With lotus in the lake and willows by the hall,
Willow leaves like her brows and lotus like her face;
At the sight of all these, how could his tears not fall?
Or when in vernal breeze were peach and plum full-blown
Or when in autumn rain parasol leaves were shed?
In Western as in Southern Court was grass o'ergrown;
With fallen leaves unswept the marble steps turned red.
Actors, although still young, began to have hair grey;
Eunuchs and waiting maids looked old in palace deep.
Fireflies flitting the hall, mutely he pined away;
The lonely lampwick burned out, still he could not sleep.

迟迟钟鼓初长夜,
耿耿星河欲曙天。
鸳鸯瓦冷霜华重,
翡翠衾寒谁与共?
悠悠生死别经年,
魂魄不曾来入梦。
临邛道士鸿都客①,
能以精诚致魂魄。
为感君王辗转思,
遂教方士②殷勤觅。
排空驭气③奔如电,
升天入地求之遍。
上穷碧落④下黄泉,
两处茫茫皆不见。
忽闻海上有仙山,
山在虚无缥缈间。
楼阁玲珑五云起,
其中绰约多仙子。

① 临邛(qióng)道士鸿都客: 意为长安有个从临邛来的道士; 鸿都, 东汉都城洛阳的宫门名, 此处借指长安。

② 方士: 有法术的人, 指道士。

③ 排空驭气: 即腾云驾雾。

④ 碧落: 指天上。

Slowly beat drums and rang bells, night began to grow long;
Bright shone the Starry Stream; daybreak seemed to come late.
The lovebird tiles grew chilly with hoarfrost so strong;
His kingfisher quilt was cold, not shared by a mate.
One long, long year the dead with the living was parted;
Her soul came not in dreams to see the broken-hearted.
A Taoist sorcerer came to the palace door,
Skilled to summon the spirits from the other shore.
Moved by the monarch's yearning for the departed fair,
He was ordered to seek for her everywhere.
Borne on the air, like flash of lightning flew,
In heaven and on earth he searched through and through.
Up to the azure vault and down to deepest place,
Nor above nor below could he e'er find her trace.
He learned that on the sea were fairy mountains proud,
Which now appeared now disappeared amid the cloud
Of rainbow colors, where rose magnificent bowers
And dwelt so many fairies as graceful as flowers.

中有一人字太真，
雪肤花貌参差是。
金阙西厢叩玉扃①，　　　　　　　① 玉扃(jiōng)：玉门。
转教小玉报双成。
闻道汉家天子使，
九华帐里梦魂惊。
揽衣推枕起徘徊，
珠箔银屏迤逦②开。　　　　　　　② 迤(yǐ)逦(lǐ)：接连不断地。
云鬓半偏新睡觉③，　　　　　　　③ 新睡觉(jué)：刚睡醒；觉，醒。
花冠不整下堂来。
风吹仙袂④飘飘举，　　　　　　　④ 袂(mèi)：衣袖。
犹似霓裳羽衣舞。
玉容寂寞⑤泪阑干⑥，　　　　　　⑤ 玉容寂寞：神色黯淡凄楚。
梨花一枝春带雨。　　　　　　　　⑥ 阑干：纵横交错的样子，此处形容泪痕。
含情凝睇⑦谢君王，　　　　　　　⑦ 凝睇(dì)：凝视，注视。
一别音容两渺茫。　　　　　　　　⑧ 昭阳殿：汉成帝宠妃赵飞燕的宫殿，此处借指杨贵妃曾经的寝宫。
昭阳殿⑧里恩爱绝，
蓬莱宫⑨中日月长。　　　　　　　⑨ 蓬莱宫：蓬莱为传说中的海上仙山，此处指杨贵妃在仙山的居所。

Among them was a queen whose name was Ever True;
Her snow-white skin and sweet face might afford a clue.
Knocking at western gate of palace hall, he bade
The fair porter to inform the queen's waiting maid.
When she heard that there came the monarch's embassy,
The queen was startled out of dreams in her canopy.
Pushing aside the pillow, she rose and got dressed,
Passing through silver screen and pearl shade to meet the guest.
Her cloud-like hair awry, not full awake at all,
Her flowery cap slanted, she came into the hall.
The wind blew up her fairy sleeves and made them float
As if she danced still *Rainbow Skirt and Feathered Coat*.
Her jade-white face crisscrossed with tears in lonely world
Like a spray of pear blossoms in spring rain impearled.
She bade him thank her lord, lovesick and broken-hearted;
They knew nothing of each other after they parted.
Love and happiness long ended within palace walls;
Days and nights appeared long in the Fairyland halls.

回头下望人寰①处,
不见长安见尘雾。
唯将旧物表深情,
钿合金钗寄将去。
钗留一股合一扇,
钗擘②黄金合分钿。
但令心似金钿坚,
天上人间会相见。
临别殷勤重寄词,
词中有誓两心知。
七月七日长生殿,
夜半无人私语时。
在天愿作比翼鸟③,
在地愿为连理枝④。
天长地久有时尽,
此恨⑤绵绵无绝期。

① 人寰(huán):人间。

② 擘(bò):分开,意同"掰",也可读作"bāi"。

③ 比翼鸟:传说中的鸟,据说只有一目一翼,雌雄并在一起才能飞行。

④ 连理枝:两株树木的树干交缠相抱。古人常用此比喻情侣相爱、永不分离。

⑤ 恨:遗憾。

Turning her head and fixing on the earth her gaze,
She found no capital 'mid clouds of dust and haze.
To show her love was deep, she took out keepsakes old
For him to carry back, hairpin and case of gold.
Keeping one side of the case and one wing of the pin,
She sent to her lord the other half of the twin.
"If our two hearts as firm as the gold should remain,
In heaven or on earth some time we'll meet again."
At parting, she confided to the messenger
A secret vow known only to her lord and her.
On seventh day of seventh moon when none was near,
At midnight in Long Life Hall he whispered in her ear:
"On high, we'd be two birds flying wing to wing;
On earth, two trees with branches twined from spring to spring."
The boundless sky and endless earth may pass away,
But this vow unfulfilled will be regretted for aye.

赠卖松者

一束苍苍色,
知从涧底来。
斫掘①经几日,
枝叶满尘埃。
不买非他意,
城中无地栽。

① 斫(zhuó)掘:挖掘。

公元808年,有人抨击时政,触犯了宰相,不但贬官,而且牵连多人。白居易当时任左拾遗,提出谏议,未被采纳,就写了这首诗。"苍苍色"指被贬官的人,"涧底"就是山沟,比喻出身寒微。挖掘松树不易,暗示发现人才困难;松树挖掘出来之后,枝叶上满是尘埃,象征人才被埋没;松树没有人买,表示人才不受重用。"城中"隐射朝廷,朝政黑暗,人才也就无用武之地了。

For the Seller of Dwarf Pines

A bundle of dwarf pines look pale;

They come from the depth of the vale.

Dug up for only a few days,

Their twigs are dusted as in haze.

I will not buy them in the town.

Where can I plant them up or down?

上阳白发人

上阳人,上阳人,
红颜暗老白发新。
绿衣监使①守宫门,
一闭上阳多少春!
玄宗末岁初选入,
入时十六今六十。
同时采择百余人,
零落年深残此身。
忆昔吞悲别亲族,
扶入车中不教②哭。
皆云入内便承恩,
脸似芙蓉胸似玉。

① 绿衣监使:内侍省负责监视宫女的宫教等官员,唐制中着绿衣。

② 不教:不让。

《上阳白发人》是白居易《新乐府》50首中的第7首。上阳宫是唐玄宗在洛阳的行宫。玄宗派人到民间去挑选美女,但是杨贵妃专宠,怕美丽的宫女接近皇帝,就把她们派到上阳宫去。诗中的白发人是一个16岁入宫的妙龄少女,在深宫内院幽禁了44年,没有见过皇帝一面,只是既嫌秋夜长,又怨春日迟,天明盼着天黑,天黑又盼天明,一直盼成了白发苍苍的老人,盼望变成失望,失望又变成了绝望。这首诗写出了古代女性的悲惨命运。

The White-haired Palace Maid

The Shangyang Palace maid, the Shangyang Palace maid,
Her hair grows white, her rosy cheeks grow dark and fade.
The palace gate is guarded by eunuchs in green.
How many springs have passed, immured as she has been!
She was first chosen for the imperial household
At the age of sixteen; now she's sixty years old.
The hundred beauties brought in with her have all gone,
Flickering out through long years, leaving her alone.
She swallowed grief when she left home in days gone by,
Helped into the cab, she was forbidden to cry.
Once in the palace, she'd be favored, it was said;
Her face was fair as lotus, her bosom like jade.

未容君王得见面，
已被杨妃遥侧目①。
妒令潜配上阳宫，
一生遂向空房宿。
宿空房，秋夜长，
夜长无寐天不明。
耿耿②残灯背壁影，
萧萧暗雨打窗声。
春日迟，
日迟独坐天难暮。
宫莺百啭③愁厌闻，
梁燕双栖老休妒④。
莺归燕去长悄然，
春往秋来不记年。
唯向深宫望明月，
东西四五百回圆。
今日宫中年最老，
大家⑤遥赐尚书号。

① 遥侧目：远远地斜眼看，表示嫉妒。

② 耿耿：微弱的光亮。

③ 啭（zhuàn）：鸣叫。

④ 休妒：不再羡慕、嫉妒。

⑤ 大家：内宫对皇帝的称谓。

But to the emperor she could never come nigh,

For Lady Yang had cast on her a jealous eye.

She was consigned to Shangyang Palace full of gloom,

To pass her lonely days and nights in a bare room.

In empty chamber long seemed each autumnal night;

Sleepless in bed, it seemed she'd never see daylight.

Dim, dim the lamplight throws her shadow on the walls;

Shower by shower on her windows chill rain falls.

Spring days drag slow;

She sits alone to see light won't be dim and low.

She's tired to hear the palace orioles sing and sing,

Too old to envy pairs of swallows on the wing.

Silent, she sees the birds appear and disappear,

And counts nor springs nor autumns coming year by year.

Watching the moon o'er palace again and again,

Four hundred times and more she's seen it wax and wane.

Today the oldest honorable maid of all,

She is entitled Secretary of Palace Hall.

小头鞵履①窄衣裳,
青黛点眉眉细长。
外人不见见应笑,
天宝末年时世妆。
上阳人,苦最多。
少亦苦,老亦苦,
少苦老苦两如何?
君不见昔时吕向美人赋②,
又不见今日上阳白发歌!

① 鞵(xié)、履(lǚ):二字同义,皆是指鞋。

② 美人赋:作者自注为"天宝末,有密采艳色者,当时号花鸟使,吕向献《美人赋》以讽之。"

Her gown is tightly fitted, her shoes like pointed prows;
With dark green pencil she draws long, long slender brows.
Seeing her, outsiders would even laugh with tears;
Her old-fashioned dress has been out of date for years.
The Shangyang maid, to suffer is her fate, all told;
She suffered while still young; she suffers now she's old.
Do you not know a satire spread in days gone by?
Today for white-haired Shangyang Palace maid we'll sigh.

卖炭翁

卖炭翁,

伐薪烧炭南山中。

满面尘灰烟火色①,

两鬓苍苍十指黑。

卖炭得钱何所营?

身上衣裳口中食。

可怜身上衣正单,

心忧炭贱愿天寒。

夜来城外一尺雪,

晓驾炭车辗冰辙。

① 烟火色:烟熏后的脸色,此处表现卖炭翁的辛劳。

《卖炭翁》是《新乐府》中的第32首。诗中写卖炭翁伐薪烧炭,两鬓苍苍,可见年迈;满面尘土,可见生活艰苦。"卖炭得钱何所营?身上衣裳口中食",可见他贫寒。虽然他"身上衣正单",却"心忧炭贱愿天寒",可见他多么需要卖炭赚钱来维持生计。但他千辛万苦烧出来的千余斤炭,却被宦官强征暴敛,只用"半匹红纱一丈绫"的代价,就抢走了,叫卖炭翁如何能生活下去!诗人以个别表现一般,通过卖炭翁的遭遇,揭示了封建王朝的剥削本质。

The Old Charcoal Seller

What does the old man fare?

He cuts the wood in southern hill and fires his ware.

His face is grimed with smoke and streaked with ash and dust,

His temples grizzled and his fingers all turned black.

The money earned by selling charcoal is not just

Enough for food for his mouth and clothing for his back.

Though his coat is thin, he hopes winter will set in,

For cold weather will keep up the charcoal's good price.

At night a foot of snow falls outside city walls;

At dawn his charcoal cart crushes ruts in the ice.

牛困人饥日已高,
市南门外泥中歇。
翩翩两骑来是谁?
黄衣使者① 白衫儿②。
手把文书口称敕③,
回车叱牛牵向北④。
一车炭,千余斤,
宫使驱将惜不得。
半匹红纱一丈绫⑤,
系向牛头充炭直。

① 黄衣使者:指宦官。
② 白衫儿:宦官的手下。
③ 敕(chì):皇帝的诏书或命令。
④ 牵向北:此处指牵向宫中。

⑤ 半匹红纱一丈绫:唐代商贸交易中,绢帛等丝织品可代货币使用。当时半匹纱和一丈绫,与一车炭的价值相差很远。此为官方用贱价强夺民财的体现。

The sun is high, the ox tired out and hungry he;
Outside the southern gate in snow and slush they rest.
Two riders canter up. Alas! Who can they be?
Two palace heralds in the yellow jackets dressed.
Decree in hand, which is imperial order, one says;
They turn the cart about and at the ox they shout.
A cartload of charcoal a thousand catties weighs;
They drive the cart away. What dare the old man say?
Ten feet of silk and twenty feet of gauze deep red,
That is the payment they fasten to the ox's head.

同李十一醉忆元九

花时同醉破①春愁,
醉折花枝作酒筹。
忽忆故人天际②去,
计程今日到梁州。

① 破:破除,消除。

② 天际:天地交接的地方。

公元 809 年,元稹奉命出使东川,白居易在长安,同李十一到曲江慈恩寺春游饮酒,席上怀念元稹,就写了这首诗。这时元稹正在梁州,并且写了一首《梁州梦》:"梦君同绕曲江头,也向慈恩院院游。亭吏呼人排去马,忽惊身在古梁州。"说来也巧,元稹写的梦境,居然和白居易写的真实情况相符,真是"心有灵犀一点通"了。白居易的诗是一首即景生情、因事起意、以情深意真见长的作品。

Thinking of Yuan Zhen While Drinking with Li Eleventh

We drink beneath the flowers to drown vernal grief;
I pluck a branch in blossom to write on a leaf,
Thinking of our friend who has gone far, far away;
Counting up, he must have reached Liangzhou today.

望驿台

靖安宅里当窗柳,
望驿台前扑地花。
两处春光同日尽,
居人①思客②客思家。

① 居人:留在家中的人,此处指元稹妻子。
② 客:指离家在外的元稹。

公元809年,元稹在东川写了一组绝句《使东川》,白居易也写了12首和诗,这是其中之一。第一句"靖安宅里"指元稹夫人在长安靖安宅里思念丈夫。"当窗柳"是怀念远人的意思,唐代折柳送别,柳丝柔长不断,象征情思不绝。第二句写元稹在东川驿邸,看见落花满地,自然也想起了家中的如花美眷。后两句说:到了三月三十日,两地都春尽花残,夫妇却不能重聚,只好流泪眼想流泪眼,断肠人念断肠人了。

For Roaming Yuan Zhen

Your wife gazes at yellowing willow at home;
You at flowers falling on the ground while you roam.
Spring comes to end in two places on the same day;
You think of home and she of you far, far away.

江楼月

嘉陵江曲曲江池,
明月虽同人别离。
一宵光景潜①相忆,
两地阴晴远不知。
谁料江边怀我夜,
正当池畔望君时。
今朝共语方同悔,
不解②多情先寄诗。

① 潜:表深思的神态。

② 不解:没有想到。

本诗也是白居易公元 809 年和元稹诗的作品。第一联写元稹远在东川嘉陵江边,白居易在长安曲江池畔,两人同时对月,却相距千里之遥。第二联"一宵"说明相忆时间之长,"潜"字暗示相忆之深,但是两地并不能相互沟通。第三联说:想不到元稹在嘉陵江边遥念我时,我也在曲江池畔望月怀人。第四联说:一直等到我得了元稹寄来的诗,才后悔自己为什么不早把诗寄去。全诗情景交融,看来句句抒情,其实情中有景:江楼、明月、诗人、友人,都融合在怀念之中了。

The Moon over the Riverside Tower

You stand by River Jialing, I by winding streams.
Though far apart, still we share the same bright moonbeams.
All night long I think of you and for you I pine,
For I am not sure if you see the same moon shine.
Who knows when by waterside I'm longing for you,
By nocturnal riverside you're missing me too.
When I receive your poem, I regret today:
Why did I not send mine to you so far away?

买 花

许渊冲译白居易诗选

帝城春欲暮,
喧喧①车马度。
共道牡丹时,
相随买花去。
贵贱无常价②,
酬直③看花数:
灼灼④百朵红,
戋戋⑤五束素⑥。
上张幄幕庇⑦,
旁织笆篱护。

① 喧喧:喧闹嘈杂的声音。

② 无常价:没有固定的价格。

③ 酬直:指花的价钱;直:通"值"。

④ 灼灼:形容色彩鲜艳的样子。

⑤ 戋(jiān)戋:形容堆积得很多的样子。

⑥ 五束素:古代以五匹为一束,即二十五匹白绢。

⑦ 幄幕庇:用帘幕遮挡。

这首诗通过唐代京城买牡丹花的盛况,揭露了社会矛盾的某些本质方面。暮春时,农村青黄不接,长安城中却车水马龙,忙于买花。富贵人家挥金如土,一株开了百朵花的红牡丹,估价竟相当于二十五匹帛,昂贵得惊人。一个从啼饥号寒的农村来到京城的田舍翁,看了不禁长叹,一丛花居然要花费十户中等人家的税粮。这就尖锐地反映了剥削的富人和穷苦的农民之间的深刻矛盾。

Buying Flowers

The capital's in parting spring,
Steeds run and neigh and cab bells ring.
Peonies are at their best hours
And people rush to buy the flowers.
They do not care about the price,
Just count and buy those which seem nice.
For hundred blossoms dazzling red,
Twenty-five rolls of silk they spread.
Sheltered above by curtains wide,
Protected with fences by the side,

水洒复泥封,
移来色如故。
家家习为俗,
人人迷不悟①。

有一田舍翁,
偶来买花处。
低头独长叹,
此叹无人谕②。
一丛深色花,
十户中人③赋。

① 迷不悟:迷恋于赏花,不知这是奢侈的事情。

② 谕:知晓,明白。

③ 中人:即中户,中等人家。唐代按户征收赋税,分上中下三等。

Roots sealed with mud, with water sprayed,
Removed, their beauty does not fade.
Accustomed to this way for long,
No family e'er thinks it wrong.
What's the old peasant doing there?
Why should he come to Flower Fair?
Head bowed, he utters sigh on sigh
And nobody understands why.
A bunch of deep-red peonies
Costs taxes of ten families.

惜牡丹花

惆怅①阶前红牡丹,
晚来唯有两枝残。
明朝风起应吹尽,
夜惜衰红把火看。

① 惆怅:伤感,失意。

　　白居易这首诗很出名,后来李商隐的《花下醉》"客散酒醒深夜后,更持红烛赏残花",苏东坡的《海棠》"只恐夜深花睡去,故烧高烛照红妆",可能都受到白居易这首诗的启发。《唐诗鉴赏辞典》中说:第二句"晚来唯有两枝残"是"只有两枝残败"的意思。那第一句为什么说"惆怅阶前红牡丹"呢?可见第二句是红牡丹"唯有"两残枝的意思,所以诗人才惆怅了。因为担心明日起风会把残花吹尽,所以诗人才会秉烛看残红。

The Last Look at the Peonies at Night

I'm saddened by the courtyard peonies brilliant red;

At dusk only two of them are left on their bed.

I am afraid they can't survive the morning blast;

By lantern light I take a look at the long, long last.

村 夜

霜草苍苍①虫切切,
村南村北行人绝。
独出前门望野田,
月明荞麦花如雪。

① 苍苍:苍白色。

这首诗用白描的手法写出了一个乡村之夜。"霜草苍苍"点出了秋色的浓重,虫声切切渲染了秋夜的凄清。村南村北,行人绝迹,写的是景,但是景色的萧瑟凄凉,又透露出诗人孤独寂寞的心情。后两句从门内转到野外,一望明月如水,荞麦如雪,这光明的景象和诗人忧郁的心情形成了鲜明的对比,使诗人的心灵受到大自然的洗礼,感情也变得洁如霜雪了。这种寓情于景的写法使诗读起来更富有韵味。

One Night in the Village

The chilly crickets chirp among the grass frost-white;

North and south of the village there's no man in sight.

I come outdoors alone and gaze on the fields, lo!

The buckwheat steeped in moonlight looks as white as snow.

欲与元八卜邻，先有是赠

平生心迹最相亲，
欲隐墙东①不为身。
明月好同三径②夜，
绿杨③宜作两家春。
每因暂出犹思伴，
岂得安居不择邻？
可独④终身数相见，
子孙长作隔墙人。

① 墙东：指代隐居之地。典故出自《后汉书·逸民传·逢萌》："君公遭乱独不去，侩牛自隐。时人谓之论曰：'避世墙东王君公。'"

② 三径：指代隐居之所。典故出自陶渊明《归去来兮辞》："三径就荒，松菊犹存"。

③ 绿杨：借用南朝陆慧晓与张融为邻的典故，两家中间有池，池上有绿杨，表示自己愿与元八为邻。

④ 可独：何止，不仅仅。

元八是元稹（元九）的堂兄，是白居易的诗友。公元815年，元八在长安升平坊买了一所新宅，白居易想和他结邻而居，就写了这首诗。前四句说：你我是生平最知心的朋友，都想隐居生活而不谋求自身的功名利禄。既然如此，那我们就结为邻居吧，让明月的清辉共照

On Becoming Neighbor of Yuan Eighth

In my life you are the friend nearest to my heart;
I'll live by your east wall, not to be kept apart.
The moon will shed bright rays on our pine-clad pathways;
Green willows bring to our houses the same spring days.
Even in short outings we need companions good.
How can we not, when long installed, choose neighborhood?
Now we may call on each other from spring to fall;
Our sons will never be separated by the wall.

我们的松径，让绿杨的春色回到我们两家。后四句说：暂时外出，还需要结伴同行，长期定居，怎能不选择邻居？一旦为邻，不但可以时常相见，而且子孙后代也可以和睦相处。这首诗看起来是说理，其实理中有情，写出了殷切而纯真的友谊。

燕子楼

（三首其一）

满窗明月满帘霜，
被冷灯残拂卧床①。
燕子楼中霜月夜，
秋来只为一人长。

① 拂卧床：此处暗示盼盼侍妾的身份，也表明其生活的变化。

燕子楼是唐代张尚书在彭城（今徐州）的宅第。尚书曾在宅中宴请白居易和张仲素，并请出爱伎盼盼歌舞助兴。尚书死后，盼盼誓不再嫁，在燕子楼住了十几年。张仲素对盼盼的专情不胜感慨，写了三首七绝《燕子楼》，白居易也和了三首。第一首用"满窗月"和"满帘霜"对照，把"被冷"和"灯残"合写，当年盼盼为尚书拂床，而今只为自己一人，就觉得霜晨月夜都太长了。第二首写盼盼怎样对待歌舞时穿过的衣裳。《霓裳曲》是唐玄宗时著名的舞曲，现在尚书已死，她也不再歌舞，就把舞衣叠起，让金花褪去光彩，罗衫改变颜色，只剩自己一个人流泪了。第三首中的"客"是张仲素，他去洛阳看了尚书墓，说是坟前的白杨已经高大得可以做柱子了，盼盼的红颜怎能不"蜡炬成灰泪始干"呢！诗人抚今思昔，写出了盼盼春日秋夜的相思，表达了她的一片深情。

The Pavilion of Swallows

(I)

Her room is drowned in moonlight and the screen in frost;
The quilt grows cold with dying lamp; she makes the bed.
The moonlit night in which Swallows' Pavilion's lost,
Since autumn came, lengthens for one who mourns the dead.

燕子楼

（三首其二）

钿晕罗衫色似烟，
几回欲著即潸然。
自从不舞霓裳曲，
叠在空①箱十一年。

① 空：形容精神上的空虚。

The Pavilion of Swallows

(II)

Her silken dress with golden flowers fades like smoke;
She tries to put it on, but soon she melts in tears.
Since she no longer danced to the air of "Rainbow Cloak",
It has been stored up in the chest for ten long years.

燕子楼

（三首其三）

今春有客洛阳回，
曾到尚书墓上来。
见说白杨堪作柱，
争教红粉①不成灰？

① 红粉：此处指盼盼的红颜。

The Pavilion of Swallows
(III)

Some friends coming back from ancient capital say
They've visited the grave of her dear lord again.
The graveyard poplar white grows high as pillar grey.
How can her rosy face still beautiful remain?

花 非 花

花非花,雾非雾。
夜半来,天明去。
来如春梦几多时,
去似朝云①无觅处。

① 朝云:典故出自《高唐赋》,化用"朝云暮雨",比喻男女情爱。

　　《花非花》是白居易写的一首朦胧诗,诗中人物似花似雾,如梦如云。通篇都用比喻,但是只用喻体(用作比喻之物),不见喻本(所喻之人或物),所以就朦胧了。这首诗由作者编入"感伤"之部,放在悼亡之作《真娘墓》和《简简吟》之后。《真娘墓》中有"真娘死时犹少年""难留连,易销歇;塞北花,江南雪"等三七言诗句,《简简吟》中有"彩云易散琉璃脆"之句,所以《花非花》也很可能是悼亡之作。

A Flower in the Haze

In bloom, she's not a flower;
Hazy, she's not a haze.
She comes at midnight hour;
She goes with starry rays.
She comes like vernal dreams that cannot stay;
She goes like morning clouds that melt away.

初贬官过望秦岭

草草①辞家忧后事,
迟迟去国问前途。
望秦岭上回头立,
无限秋风吹白须。

① 草草:匆忙。

公元815年,宰相武元衡被暗杀身亡,白居易上书奏请捉拿凶手,却被权贵责为越职上奏,贬为江州(今江西省九江市)司马。他路经骊山脚下的望秦岭时,写下了这首双关诗。第一句说匆匆离家,来不及安排家事,更担心的是国家大事。第二句说慢慢上路,舍不得离开国都,去江州的路途遥远,自己政治上的前途更是渺茫。所以在望秦岭上回望京城,就只感到秋风吹动白须,自己觉得茫然了。

Passing by the Head-turning Peak in Banishment

Leaving home in haste, I'm worried about my fate;
Without knowing what will happen, I linger late.
On the Head-turning Peak I look back without cease,
Letting my white beard sway in endless autumn breeze.

蓝桥驿见元九诗

蓝桥春雪君归日,
秦岭秋风我去时。
每到驿亭①先下马,
循墙绕柱觅君诗。

① 驿亭:驿站所设的供旅途休息处,古时驿站有亭。

公元815年农历正月,元稹回京城时经过蓝桥驿,在驿亭壁上留下了一首诗;三个月后,他就被贬谪到通州了。到了秋天,白居易也被贬去江州,经过蓝桥驿,读到了元稹的七律,就写了这首七绝。两人先后被贬,春雪秋风,西去东归,风尘仆仆。在人生的道路上,友情可贵,题咏可歌,共同的遭遇可泣。最后一句别开生面,用人物的行动作结:"循墙"是寸寸搜寻,"绕柱"是面面俱到,"觅诗"是转来转去。这首诗写出了诗人亲切的友情,收到了强烈的艺术效果。

Reading Yuan Zhen's Poem at Blue Bridge Post

When you came back, you passed by Blue Bridge in spring snow;
Now banished to the south, in autumn breeze I go.
Seeing a post, I dismount and enter the hall
To find your verse on the pillar along the wall.

舟中读元九诗

把君诗卷灯前读,
诗尽灯残天未明。
眼痛灭灯犹暗坐,
逆风吹浪打船声。

　　白居易被贬江州,离开长安,南下襄阳,然后坐船东去九江。他在船上伴着荧荧的灯火,读着元稹的诗卷,想着共同的遭遇,不免兴起同是天涯沦落人之感。满腔汹涌澎湃的感情,使他无法安枕;江上翻腾起伏的狂风巨浪,仿佛在为他的心情伴奏。诗中用了三个"灯"字:灯前、灯残、灭灯,灯光由高而低,风浪却由低而高,更从正反两面衬托出诗人悲愤不平的心情。

Reading Yuan Zhen's Poems on a Boat

I read your book of poetry by the lamplight,
And finish it when oil burns low at dead of night.
Eyes sore, I blow the light out and sit in the dark;
The waves brought up by adverse wind beat on the bark.

放言①

① 放言：畅所欲言。

朝真暮伪何人辨，
古往今来底事无？
但爱臧生②能诈圣，
可知宁子解佯愚③？
草萤有耀终非火，
荷露虽团岂是珠？
不取燔柴④兼照乘，
可怜光彩亦何殊！

② 臧(zāng)生：指臧武仲。

③ 佯愚：伪装愚笨。

④ 燔(fán)柴：出自《礼记·祭法》："燔柴于泰坛"，此处用作名词，意为大火。

《放言》五首是白居易贬江州途中所作，这里选的是第一首。诗中说到真假难辨，早上看来还是真的，到了晚上却又原形毕露。古往今来，什么怪事没有出过？春秋时代认为臧武仲是个圣人，孔子却揭穿他是个要挟君主的奸诈之徒；宁武子在乱世显得糊涂，其实却是大智若愚。草丛中的萤火虫虽能发光，但终究不是火；荷叶上的露珠虽然滚圆，却并不能当作珍珠。萤火既不能燃烧木柴，也不能照亮车辆，发光又有什么用？诗人就这样用形象和典故畅所欲言，说明了自己直言取祸的道理。

Written at Random

It turns out false at dusk though at dawn it seemed true.

Is there from olden days to now anything new?

All call the powerful hypocrite a saint cool.

Who knows the wise man may pretend to be a fool?

The light sent out by fireflies is not fire amid grass;

Round dewdrops on lotus leaves are not pearls, alas!

If fire cannot burn and illuminate the car,

Fireflies are bright and dewdrops are round as pearls are.

琵琶行

浔阳江①头夜送客,
枫叶荻花秋瑟瑟。
主人下马客在船,
举酒欲饮无管弦。
醉不成欢惨将别,
别时茫茫江浸月。
忽闻水上琵琶声,
主人忘归客不发。
寻声暗问弹者谁?
琵琶声停欲语迟。

① 浔阳江:据考证为流经浔阳城的溢水,即江西省九江市北的龙开河(1997年被人工填埋)。

《琵琶行》和《长恨歌》一样,也是白居易的传世名作。早在作者生前,已经是"童子解吟长恨曲,胡儿能唱琵琶篇"了。作者在诗中写自己从长安被贬到九江之后,在江边送客时,听到船上的歌女弹奏琵琶,诉说天涯沦落之恨,就同客人登船听乐。但是琵琶女"千呼万唤始出来",因为她有话不便明说,也不愿意见人,只是借琵琶来揭示自己的内心世界。所以她弹奏的乐曲"似诉平生不得意","说尽心中无限事"。

Song of a Pipa Player

One night by riverside I bade a friend goodbye;
In maple leaves and rushes autumn seemed to sigh.
My friend and I dismounted and came into the boat;
We wished to drink but there was no music afloat.
Without flute songs we drank our cups with heavy head;
The moonbeams blended with water when we were to part.
Suddenly o'er the stream we heard a pipa sound;
I forgot to go home and the guest stood spellbound.
We followed where the music led to find the player,
But heard the pipa stop and no music in the air.

作者借助语言的音韵摹写音乐,用各种生动的比喻来加强形象性,如"大珠小珠落玉盘"就是用视觉形象来显露听觉形象;又如"别有幽愁暗恨生,此时无声胜有声",更描绘了余音袅袅、余味无穷的艺术境界。这样,作者通过音乐形象的千变万化,展现了琵琶女起伏回荡的心潮。最后,作者更写琵琶女自诉身世,详昔而略今;写自己的遭遇,则详今而略昔。这样,他又使两个天涯沦落人的遗恨,一同流传千古了。

移船相近邀相见,
添酒回灯①重开宴。

① 回灯:重新点亮灯光。

千呼万唤始出来,
犹抱琵琶半遮面。
转轴拨弦三两声,
未成曲调先有情。
弦弦掩抑②声声思③,
似诉平生不得志。

② 掩抑:压抑。
③ 思(sì):悲伤的思绪。

低眉信手续续弹,
说尽心中无限事。
轻拢慢捻抹复挑,
初为《霓裳》后《六幺》④。

④《六幺》:唐代著名歌舞曲,又名《录要》《绿腰》《乐世》。

大弦嘈嘈如急雨,
小弦切切如私语。
嘈嘈切切错杂弹,
大珠小珠落玉盘。

We moved our boat towards the one whence came the strain,
Brought back the lamp, asked for more wine and drank again.
Repeatedly we called for the fair player till
She came, her face half hidden behind a pipa still.
She turned the pegs and tested twice or thrice each string;
Before a tune was played we heard her feelings sing.
Each string she plucked, each note she struck with pathos strong,
All seemed to say she'd missed her dreams all her life long.
Head bent, she played with unpremeditated art
On and on to pour out her overflowing heart.
She lightly plucked, slowly stroked and twanged loud
The song of *Green Waist* after that of *Rainbow Cloud*.
The thick strings loudly thrummed like the pattering rain;
The fine strings softly tinkled in a murmuring strain.
When mingling loud and soft notes were together played,
You heard large and small pearls cascade on plate of jade.

间关①莺语花底滑,
幽咽②泉流冰下难③。
冰泉冷涩弦凝绝④,
凝绝不通声暂歇。
别有幽愁暗恨生,
此时无声胜有声。
银瓶乍破水浆迸,
铁骑突出刀枪鸣。
曲终收拨当心画,
四弦一声如裂帛。
东船西舫悄无言,
唯见江心秋月白。
沉吟放拨插弦中,
整顿衣裳起敛容⑤。
自言本是京城女,
家在虾蟆陵⑥下住。

① 间(jiàn)关: 鸟鸣声,莺语流转为"间关"。
② 幽咽: 阻塞不畅。
③ 冰下难: 泉流冰下阻塞难通,形容弦声由流畅转为冷涩。
④ 凝绝: 凝滞。

⑤ 敛容: 神情庄重的样子。

⑥ 虾(há)蟆陵: 长安城东南,曲江附近。

Now you heard orioles warble in flowery land,
Then a sobbing stream run along a beach of sand.
But the stream seemed so cold as to tighten the string;
From tightened strings no more sound could be heard to sing.
Still we heard hidden grief and vague regret concealed;
Then music expressed far less than silence revealed.
Suddenly we heard water burst a silver jar,
And the clash of spears and sabres come from afar.
She made a central sweep when the music was ending;
The four strings made one sound, as of silk one was rending.
Silence reigned left and right of the boat, east and west;
We saw but autumn moon white in the river's breast.
She slid the plectrum pensively between the strings,
Smoothed out her dress and rose with a composed mien.
"I spent," she said, "in the capital my early springs,
Where at the foot of Mount of Toads my home had been.

十三学得琵琶成,
名属教坊①第一部。
曲罢曾教善才服,
妆成每被秋娘②妒。
五陵年少争缠头③,
一曲红绡④不知数。
钿头银篦⑤击节碎,
血色罗裙翻酒污。
今年欢笑复明年,
秋月春风等闲⑥度。
弟走从军阿姨死,
暮去朝来颜色故⑦。
门前冷落鞍马稀,
老大嫁作商人妇。
商人重利轻别离,
前月浮梁⑧买茶去。

① 教坊:唐代管理宫廷乐队、教练歌舞的官方机构。

② 秋娘:唐代歌舞伎常用的名号,此处泛指艺高貌美的歌伎。

③ 缠头:用锦帛缠住乐舞者的头,以示奖赏。

④ 绡(xiāo):精致的丝织品。

⑤ 钿(diàn)头银篦(bì):镶嵌着精美花钿的篦形发饰;篦,梳子。

⑥ 等闲:随随便便,形容虚度光阴。

⑦ 颜色故:容颜老去。

⑧ 浮梁:地名,唐属饶州。

At thirteen I learned on the pipa how to play,

And my name was among the primas of the day.

I won my master's admiration for my skill;

My beauty was envied by songstresses fair still.

The gallant young men vied to shower gifts on me;

One tune played, countless silk rolls were given with glee.

Beating time, I let silver comb and pin drop down,

And spilt-out wine oft stained my blood-red silken gown.

From year to year I laughed my joyous life away

On moonlit autumn night as windy vernal day.

My younger brother left for war, and died my maid;

Days passed, nights came, and my beauty began to fade.

Fewer and fewer were cabs and steeds at my door;

I married a smug merchant when my prime was o'er.

The merchant cared for money much more than for me;

One month ago he went away to purchase tea,

去来①江口守空船,
绕船月明江水寒。
夜深忽梦少年事,
梦啼妆泪红阑干。
我闻琵琶已叹息,
又闻此语重唧唧②。
同是天涯沦落人,
相逢何必曾相识!
我从去年辞帝京,
谪居卧病浔阳城。
浔阳地僻无音乐,
终岁不闻丝竹声。
住近湓江地低湿,
黄芦苦竹绕宅生。
其间旦暮闻何物?
杜鹃啼血猿哀鸣。

① 去来:离别后;来,语气助词。

② 唧唧:叹息声。

Leaving his lonely wife alone in empty boat;
Shrouded in moonlight, on the cold river I float.
Deep in the night I dreamed of happy bygone years,
And woke to find my rouged face crisscrossed with tears."
Listening to her sad music, I sighed with pain;
Hearing her story, I sighed again and again.
Both of us in misfortune go from shore to shore.
Meeting now, need we have known each other before?
"I was banished from the capital last year
To live degraded and ill in this city here.
The city's too remote to know melodious song,
So I have never heard music all the year long.
I dwell by riverbank on a low and damp ground
In a house with wild reeds and stunted bamboos around.
What is here to be heard from daybreak till nightfall
But gibbon's cry and cuckoo's homeward-going call?

春江花朝秋月夜,
往往取酒还独倾。
岂无山歌与村笛?
呕哑嘲哳①难为听。
今夜闻君琵琶语,
如听仙乐耳暂②明。
莫辞更坐弹一曲,
为君翻作《琵琶行》。
感我此言良久立,
却坐③促弦弦转急。
凄凄不似向前声④,
满座重闻皆掩泣。
座中泣下谁最多?
江州司马青衫⑤湿!

① 呕哑(zhāo)哳(zhā):形容声音嘈杂。

② 暂:突然。

③ 却坐:坐回到原处。

④ 向前声:之前弹奏过的曲调。

⑤ 青衫:唐朝官服颜色由官阶决定,白居易当时官阶低,着青衫。

By blooming riverside and under autumn moon
I've often taken wine up and drunk it alone.
Though I have mountain songs and village pipes to hear,
Yet they are crude and strident and grate on the ear.
Listening to you playing on pipa tonight,
With your music divine e'en my hearing seems bright.
Will you sit down and play for us a tune once more?
I'll write for you an ode to the pipa I adore."
Touched by what I said, the player stood for long,
Then sat down, tore at strings and played another song.
So sad, so drear, so different, it moved us deep;
Those who heard it hid their face and began to weep.
Of all the company at table who wept most?
It was none other than the exiled blue-robed host.

南 浦 别

南浦凄凄别,
西风袅袅秋。
一看肠一断,
好去莫回头。

白居易在《琵琶行》序中说:"元和十年(815),予左迁九江郡司马。明年秋,送客湓浦口。"这首《南浦别》有可能是和《琵琶行》同时的作品。第一句形容内心的凄凉愁苦。第二句描写秋景的萧瑟暗淡,"袅袅"二字使风声如泣如诉,更衬托出离别的"凄凄"之情。离人已经登舟而去,但还频频回首,每一回首,都引起送行人"肠一断",所以反劝离人不要回首。这就写出了依依惜别的深情。

Farewell by Southern Riverside

By Southern Riverside we bid dreary goodbye;
Autumn seems desolate to hear the west wind sigh.
My heart would break each time you look back to the shore.
Go on before and don't turn your head any more!

大林寺桃花

人间^①四月芳菲尽,
山寺桃花始盛开。
长恨^②春归无觅处,
不知^③转入此中来。

① 人间:指庐山脚下的村落。

② 长恨:常常惋惜、遗憾。

③ 不知:岂料,意想不到。

    大林寺在庐山香炉峰顶。这首诗是白居易于公元817年初夏所作。农历四月,平地上的桃花已经凋谢,作者登到高山古寺之中,不料却看到了一片盛开的桃花。这是山高地深、时节绝晚的景象,但作者却写出了感情上的飞跃,仿佛是从现实世界进入了仙境似的。在仙境中,作者用桃花代替抽象的春光,又把春光拟人化。这样就使本诗立意新颖,构思灵巧,启人深思,惹人喜爱,是唐人绝句中的珍品。

Peach Blossoms in the Temple of Great Forest

All flowers in late spring have fallen far and wide,
But peach blossoms are full-blown on the mountainside.
I oft regret spring's gone without leaving its trace;
I didn't know how it's come up to adorn this place.

遗 爱 寺

弄①石临溪坐,
寻花绕寺行。
时时闻鸟语,
处处是泉声。

① 弄:在手中玩弄。

遗爱寺在庐山香炉峰下,离白居易所建的草堂很近。这首小诗通过临溪弄石、绕寺寻花、时时闻鸟、处处听泉等几个乘兴漫游的活动,把读者带到一个令人神往的境界。诗着重的是从动中写景,从景中抒情。

Temple of Dear Memories

Playing with pebbles, I sit by the brook;
Seeking for flowers, I turn temple's nook.
From time to time birds sing in mountains;
From place to place I hear bubbling fountains.

问刘十九

绿蚁新醅①酒,
红泥小火炉。
晚来天欲雪,
能饮一杯无②?

① 醅(pēi):酿造。

② 无:义同"否"。

这首小诗可以说是约朋友来家小饮的邀请信。酒是新酿的,没有滤清时,酒渣会浮上来,颜色微绿,好像蚂蚁似的,所以叫作绿蚁。红色泥炉小巧朴实,炉火上升,映衬着泡沫浮动的绿酒,显得分外温暖;加上外面天要下雪,更显得室内温暖如春。这时作者想到邀请刘十九来共饮一杯,使红炉绿酒温暖友人的心,而温暖的友情又使寒室生春了。

An Invitation

My new brew gives green glow;
My red clay stove flames up.
At dusk it threatens snow.
Won't you come for a cup?

夜 雪

已讶①衾枕②冷,
复见窗户明。
夜深知雪重,
时闻折竹声③。

① 讶:惊讶。
② 衾(qīn)枕:被子和枕头。
③ 折竹声:大雪压断竹子的声音。

咏雪诗写夜雪的不多,因为夜色深沉,雪光迷蒙,看不清楚,不好描写。但白居易从感觉入手,先写寒冷,这就不但点出了雪,而且暗示雪大。然后诗人才转入视觉的角度,但又不直接写雪,而是间接写窗,窗明自然表示雪下得大,积得深。前两句都写人,又处处点出了雪。后两句变换角度,转从听觉来写,听见积雪压断竹枝,可见雪势有增无已;同时说明了诗人一夜未眠,反映了他谪居江州时的孤寂心情。

Snowing at Night

Surprised to feel my quilt and pillow cold,

I wake up but to see the window bright.

Heavy with snow, I know night has grown old;

At times I hear bamboos snapped by snow white.

钟陵饯送

翠幕红筵①高在云,
歌钟一曲万家闻。
路人指点滕王阁②,
看送忠州白使君③。

① 翠幕红筵:翠绿的帐幕,红锦铺设的筵席。

② 滕王阁:位于今江西省南昌市赣江东岸,与黄鹤楼、岳阳楼并称"江南三大名楼"。

③ 使君:古时对州郡长官的尊称。

　　这首诗是白居易离开江州后,友人在滕王阁为他送行,他所写下的饯别诗。王勃的滕王阁诗早已闻名天下,"滕王高阁临江渚",白居易只用"高在云"三字虚写;"佩玉鸣鸾罢歌舞","画栋朝飞南浦云,珠帘暮卷西山雨",白诗只用"翠幕红筵"四字概括;而"歌钟一曲万家闻"则是王诗"歌舞"的扩大;"路人指点滕王阁",这才转入正题,而王诗却是开门见山;最后一句"看送忠州白使君",还是从路人观点来写饯别。总之,这首诗用高阁之盛、饯别之欢,来反衬当年江州生活的孤寂。

Farewell Feast at Zhongling

Green curtains veil the crimson hall high in the cloud;
With thrilling farewell songs a thousand houses are loud.
Passersby lending their ears point to Prince Teng's Tower
And see officials bid me adieu in the bower.

李白墓[①]

[①] 李白墓：现位于安徽省马鞍山市当涂县城东南的青山西麓，元和十二年（817年）由城南龙山东麓迁葬至此。

采石江边李白坟，
绕田无限草连云。
可怜[②]荒垄穷泉骨，
曾有惊天动地文。
但是诗人多薄命，
就中[③]沦落不过君。

[②] 可怜：可悲，可叹。

[③] 就中：其中，当中。

李白墓在采石矶江边，采石矶原名牛渚矶，是牛渚山突出长江的部分形成的。李白墓的周围一片荒凉，无边无际的野草从山下的田边一直延伸到天边。第三句的"荒垄"指荒芜的坟墓，"穷泉"就是黄泉，指埋葬人的地下。第四句说，李白的诗"笔落惊风雨，诗成泣鬼神"。第五句说，只可惜诗人的命运不好。第六句说，诗人中没有比李白更落魄的了。全诗对李白做了极高的评价，对诗人身后的萧条表示了深切的同情和不平。

Li Bai's Grave

By riverside near Rocky Hill Li Bai's grave stands;
The boundless grassland round the fields blends with the cloud.
What a pity his bones are buried in wastelands!
With his earth-shaking poems the world was loud.
There is no poet but suffers a bitter fate;
Beside Li Bai no one can say he's unfortunate!

后宫词

泪湿罗巾梦不成,
夜深前殿按歌声①。
红颜未老恩先断,
斜倚熏笼②坐到明。

① 按歌声:按照歌声的韵律打节拍。

② 熏笼:覆罩香炉的竹笼,古时一种烘烤和取暖的用具,用来熏衣被等。

　　这首诗是代宫女所作的怨词。第一句"泪湿罗巾"写宫女等待君王不来,哭得泪眼不干,这是怨的外形,是第一层怨。等待的结果是失望,只好寻梦,梦又不成,这是第二层怨。梦不成却听见前殿歌声,说明君王正在寻欢作乐,但是没有自己陪伴,这是第三层怨。如果自己年龄大了,失宠倒也情有可原,偏偏红颜未老,这是第四层怨。如果从来没有受过恩宠倒也罢了,偏偏是受宠之后恩断,这是第五层怨。恩断还不死心,却要斜倚熏笼一直等到天明,这是第六层怨。全诗由希望转到失望,由失望转到苦望,由苦望最后转到绝望;由现实进入幻想,由幻想进入痴想,由痴想再回到现实,千回百转,倾注了诗人对宫女的深挚同情。

The Deserted

Her handkerchief soaked with tears, she cannot fall asleep,

But overhears band music waft when night is deep.

Her rosy face outlasts the favor of the king;

She leans on her perfumed bed till morning birds sing.

夜 筝

紫袖红弦明月中,
自弹自感①暗低容②。
弦凝指咽声停处,
别有深情一万重。

① 自弹自感:弹筝人被自己曲中的情思所感染。
② 暗低容:愁容满面、低头沉吟的样子。

《夜筝》可以说是把《琵琶行》剪裁成了一首绝句。第一句的"紫袖"代弹筝人,"红弦"代筝,暗示她的乐伎身份,衣饰美好,乐器精良;"明月"表示是夜,可以使人想起"浔阳江头夜送客"的情景。第二句的"自弹"使人想起"低眉信手续续弹","自感"则是沉浸在乐曲中。第三句的"弦凝"使人想到"冰泉冷涩弦凝绝","指咽"则会使人想到"幽咽泉流冰下难",所以使人觉得"别有深情一万重"了。

Lute Playing at Night

In moonlight violet sleeves caress the lute red;
Playing alone and moved, she lowers and hides her head.
Her fingers sob when music stops on congealed strings,
But you can hear ten thousand songs her deep heart sings.

勤政楼^①西老柳

① 勤政楼：位于长安兴庆宫西南，始建于开元八年（720年）。

半朽临风树，

多情立马人。

开元^②一枝柳，

长庆二年^③春。

② 开元：唐玄宗年号，公元713年至741年。

③ 长庆二年：唐穆宗李恒在位第二年，即公元822年。

    勤政楼西边的老柳树是唐玄宗开元年间（713—741）种的，到了长庆二年（822），已经有100年左右的历史了。当时白居易51岁，也是半朽之人，见了半朽之树，所以立马良久，凝望出神，处在物我交融的境界。前两句用画笔勾勒了一幅临风立马图，语短情长，意境苍茫；后两句用史笔补叙了柳树和诗人的年龄，隐含了百年变迁、自然变化、人世沧桑的感慨在内，是一幅充满了感情的生活小照。

The Old Willow Tree West of the Administrative Hall

In breeze stands a half-withered tree;

Looking at it on horse has oldened me.

The tree's seen ups and downs for years;

For fifty-one springs I've shed tears.

暮江吟[①]

[①] 暮江吟：傍晚时分在江边所写的诗。

一道残阳铺水中，
半江瑟瑟[②] 半江红。
可怜[③] 九月初三夜，
露似真珠月似弓。

[②] 瑟瑟：本意为碧色宝石，此处形容江水呈碧绿色。

[③] 可怜：可爱。

这首诗大约是公元822年白居易赴杭州任刺史途中的作品。第一句说残阳照射在江面上，不说"照"而说"铺"，因为落日已经接近地平线，几乎贴近水面，仿佛铺在江上一样，一个"铺"字用得很形象化。第二句说江面皱起波纹，受光多的部分呈现一片红色，受光少的部分呈现深深的碧绿色。前两句写日落，后两句写月出。新月如弓，圆露似珠，似乎也反映出诗人在江州时的落日心态和去杭州途中轻松愉快的新月心情。

Sunset and Moonrise on the River

The departing sunbeams pave a way on the river;
Half of its waves turn red and the other half shiver.
How I love the third night of the ninth moon aglow!
The dewdrops look like pearls, the crescent like a bow.

寒闺怨

寒月沉沉洞房静,
真珠①帘外梧桐影。　　　　　①真珠:珍珠。
秋霜欲下手先知,
灯底裁缝剪刀冷。

　　唐代的府兵制规定:兵士自备衣装,衣服破损,要由家中寄来补充更换,特别是御寒的冬衣。诗中第一句的"洞房"指的是房屋后部女眷的居室。居所本已深邃,寒月一照,更见幽静;帘外梧桐投影,更见阴沉。室内的妻子正在灯下为远戍不归的征夫缝制寒衣,一摸剪刀,立刻感到秋凉;再想到远在边地受寒的丈夫,怎能不牵肠挂肚呢?全诗不言怨而怨自见,流露出作者对征夫怨妇的同情。

A Wife's Grief in Autumn

The cool moon shivers over her bower tranquil,

Outside the pearly screen the shadow of a parasol old.

Before autumn frost falls her fingers feel the chill,

When she cuts clothes by lamplight with scissors cold.

钱塘湖春行

孤山寺北贾亭西,
水面初平①云脚低②。
几处早莺争暖树,
谁家新燕啄春泥。
乱花渐欲迷人眼,
浅草才能没马蹄③。
最爱湖东行不足④,
绿杨阴⑤里白沙堤。

① 水面初平:湖水刚刚和堤岸齐平,形容春水初涨。
② 云脚低:浮云很低,看上去与湖面的水波连成一片。
③ 没(mò)马蹄:遮没马蹄。
④ 行不足:多次游览也不够;足,满足。
⑤ 阴:同"荫",树荫。

这首诗是公元823年或824年春天,白居易任杭州刺史时的作品。钱塘湖就是西湖,后湖和外湖之间的孤山寺和贾公亭,都是湖中的登临胜地。在水色天光的苍茫中,白云和湖面上荡漾的波澜连成了一片。"几处早莺",可见并不是处处的黄莺都在争夺向阳的暖树;"谁家新燕",

On Lake Qiantang in Spring

West of Pavilion Jia and north of Lonely Hill,
Water brims level with the bank and clouds hang low.
Disputing for sunny trees, early orioles trill;
Pecking vernal mud in, young swallows come and go.
A riot of blooms begin to dazzle the eye;
Amid short grass the horse hooves can barely be seen.
I love best the east of the lake under the sky:
The bank paved with white sand is shaded by willows green.

可见并不是家家燕子都在啄泥衔草，营建新巢。新开的花快要使人眼花缭乱，短短的绿草刚能遮没马蹄。这四句说明时间是早春。而最令人流连忘返的，还是绿柳掩映下的白沙堤。这首诗从"孤山寺"写起，到"白沙堤"结束，从点到面，又从面回到点，章法变化，条理井然，是写西湖的名篇。

春题湖上

湖上春来似画图,
乱峰①围绕水平铺。
松排山面千重翠,
月点波心一颗珠。
碧毯线头②抽早稻,
青罗裙带展新蒲。
未能抛得杭州去,
一半勾留③是此湖。

① 乱峰:参差错乱的山峰。

② 线头:此处指地毯上的绒毛。

③ 勾留:留恋,不舍。

这首诗作于公元824年春天,作者杭州刺史任期将满之时。第一句是总评。第二句说西湖三面环山,峰峦错落,湖水平静地铺展在群山之间。第三句说山上松树成排,重峦叠翠。第四句说月亮映在湖心,好像一颗珍珠。第五句说早稻长满株,绿油油的一片,犹如绿色的地毯。第六句说新长出的嫩绿细长的蒲叶,就像罗裙的青带子一样迎风飘动。最后两句说诗人舍不得离开杭州,一半原因是为了西湖,可见作者对杭州西湖的情深意长。

The Lake in Spring

What a charming picture when spring comes to the lake!
Amid the rugged peaks water's smooth without a break.
Hills upon hills are green with thousands of pine trees,
The moon looks like a pearl swimming in waves with ease.
Like a green carpet early paddy fields undulate,
New rushes spread out as silk girdle fascinate.
From fair Hangzhou I cannot tear myself away,
On half my heart this lake holds an alluring sway.

西湖晚归回望孤山寺赠诸客

柳湖①松岛莲花寺,
晚动归桡②出道场。
卢橘子③低山雨重④,
栟榈叶战水风凉。
烟波澹荡⑤摇空碧,
楼殿参差倚夕阳。
到岸请君回首望,
蓬莱宫在海中央。

① 柳湖:西湖周边多柳树,故称"柳湖"。
② 归桡(ráo):归船;桡,本意为船桨。
③ 卢橘子:又名"给客橙",与橘子近似。
④ 重(zhòng):沉重。
⑤ 澹(dàn)荡:荡漾,使人舒畅。

白居易在杭州时,常同宾客去垂柳掩映的西湖,青松劲立的孤山,莲花盛开的寺院,听僧侣在佛殿讲经,直到傍晚才离开庙堂,坐船回城。途中看到雨后的卢橘的果实把枝压得低垂下来,栟榈树高叶大,俨若凉扇遮径,清风一起,阔叶颤动,似乎感到了水风的清凉。在宽阔的湖面

Looking Back at the Lonely Hill on My Way across West Lake

From Lotus Temple, isle of pines in willow-girt lake,
The guests come out at dusk the oarsmen's boat to take.
After the rain, loquats hang heavy on the trees,
The waterside palm leaves shiver in the cool breeze.
The misty waves seem to blend with the azure sky,
The setting sun reddens pavilions low and high.
Will you, on reaching the shore, turn your head to see
The fairy palaces in the midst of the sea?

上,轻轻的寒烟似有似无,蓝蓝的湖波共长天一色。随着山势高下而建筑的佛寺楼殿,在夕阳残照下,金光明灭,仿佛神话中的海上蓬莱仙山,而孤山寺中又有蓬莱阁,更使佛地有如仙境。这首诗句句写景,句句含情,给人以情景交融的快感。

杭州春望

望海楼明照曙霞,
护江堤^①白踏晴沙。
涛声夜入伍员^②庙,
柳色春藏苏小家。
红袖织绫夸柿蒂,
青旗沽酒趁梨花。
谁开湖寺西南路?
草绿裙腰一道斜。

① 护江堤:指白沙堤,后人为纪念白居易称白堤。

② 伍员:字子胥,春秋时期楚国人。父兄皆被楚平王杀害,辗转逃往吴国,他协助吴王先后打败楚国、越国,然而吴王夫差听信谗言,将其杀害。

　　这首诗是白居易写杭州春景之作。第一联写登楼远望海天瑰丽的景色,旭日东升,霞光万道;钱塘江水,奔流入海;护江长堤,闪着银光。据民间传说,伍子胥因为怨恨吴王,死后驱水为涛,所以第二联说,夜里听见庙中涛声,分外清晰。苏小小是南齐钱塘名妓,这里的"苏小家"代指歌楼舞榭,掩藏在一片青青柳色之中。第三联的"红袖"指织绫的

Spring View in Hangzhou

Viewed from the Seaside Tower morning clouds look bright,
Along the river bank I tread on fine sand white.
The General's Temple hears roaring nocturnal tide,
Spring dwells in the Beauty's Bower green willows hide.
The red sleeves weave brocade broidered with flowers fine,
Blue streamers show amid pear blossoms a shop of wine.
Who opens a southwest road to the temple scene?
It slants like a silk girdle around a skirt green.

女子,"柿蒂"指绫花纹,"青旗"就是酒旗,代指酒店,"趁梨花"是说,正好赶在梨花开时去饮梨花春酒。最后一联转到西湖,"湖寺"指孤山寺,"西南路"指白堤,白堤在一片碧绿的湖洲之中,望之有如裙腰。这首诗写景结合咏古,把自然景色和风物人情结合起来,使景物更加丰富多彩,更加富有诗味。

别州民

耆老^①遮归路,
壶浆满别筵。
甘棠^②无一树,
那得泪潸然?
税重多贫户,
农饥足旱田。
唯留一湖水,
与汝救凶年^③。

① 耆(qí)老：六十称耆，七十称老，指六七十岁的老人。

② 甘棠：典故来自西周时期的开国功臣召公。相传他德政仁爱，出巡时为避免惊扰百姓，曾在一棵甘棠树下公正无私地听讼断案，后人遂以甘棠树作为颂扬官员政德之词。

③ 凶年：干旱灾荒之年。

这首诗作于公元824年5月，是作者离开杭州时的告别诗。"耆老"指60岁以上的老人，连他们都舍不得作者离开，拦住了他的去路，带来了盛满酒浆的壶和碗，摆下了送别的酒席。作者自谦不是在甘棠树下的草屋里听讼断案的清官，哪里值得老百姓这样感恩戴德，甚至感动得

Farewell to the People of Hangzhou

Old and young people bar my way,

Feast tables piled with wine and tray.

I've planted for you no pear tree.

Why should you weep to part with me?

Heavy taxes make you poor grow;

Barren fields make you hungry go.

I leave you only a lake clear

For you to pass a famine year.

流泪呢? 自己不过是怕捐税太重,百姓要过贫穷的日子,担心田地受旱,农民又要挨饿,所以就在钱塘门外修堤贮水,以防旱灾的威胁而已。这首诗写出了作者对人民的深情厚谊以及和群众的鱼水之情。

白 云 泉

天平山上白云泉,
云自无心水自闲。
何必奔冲山下去?
更添波浪向人间!

白云泉号称"吴中第一水",在苏州市西二十里的天平山中。这首诗是白居易于公元825年任苏州刺史期间所作。诗中写到白云随风飘荡,舒卷自如,无牵无挂;泉水深深潺流,自由奔泻,从容自得。诗人强调云水的自由自在、自得其乐,逍遥而惬意,有一种清静无为、与世无争的思想。所以他问清清的泉水,何必向山下奔腾飞泻而去,给纷扰多事的人间推波助澜?这首诗集中反映了诗人随遇而安、出世归隐的思想,表现了他人生观的一个侧面。

White Cloud Fountain

Behold the White Cloud Fountain on the Sky-blue Mountain!
White clouds enjoy free pleasure; water enjoys leisure.
Why should the torrent dash down from the mountain high
And overflow the human world with waves far and nigh?

秋雨夜眠

凉冷三秋①夜,
安闲一老翁。
卧迟灯灭后,
睡美雨声中。
灰宿②温瓶火,
香添暖被笼。
晓③晴寒未起,
霜叶满阶红。

① 三秋:即秋天。七月为孟秋,八月为仲秋,九月为季秋,合称三秋。

② 宿(xiǔ):夜。

③ 晓:拂晓,刚刚天亮的时候。

这首诗大约是公元832年,60岁的白居易任河南尹时所作。第一句用气候给人的"凉冷"感来形容深秋之夜。第二句刻画出一个安适闲淡的老人形象。老人不喜欢早上床,免得半夜醒来;因为心无所虑,所以在雨夜睡得安稳,一直睡到烘瓶里的燃料化为灰烬,还要烧香使被笼温暖。第二天早晨虽然晴了,但是寒气未消,不久前还红似二月花的树叶,一夜之间就被秋风秋雨无情地扫得飘零满阶。诗中反映了诗人暮年政治上心灰意懒,生活上孤寂闲散的状况。

Sleeping on a Rainy Autumn Night

Cold, cold late autumn night,
An old, old man with ease
Puts out the candlelight,
Sleeps to hear rain and breeze.
Ashes keep fire awake;
Incense perfumes the bed.
He won't rise at daybreak;
Maple leaves dye steps red.

与梦得沽酒①闲饮且约后期②

① 沽酒:买酒。
② 后期:后会之期,再次相聚的日期。

少时犹不忧生计,
老后谁能惜酒钱?
共把十千③沽一斗,
相看七十欠三年。
闲征雅令穷经史,
醉听清吟胜管弦。
更待菊黄④家酿熟,
共君一醉一陶然⑤。

③ 十千:十千钱,极言酒价之高以表二人尽兴豪饮。

④ 菊黄:菊花盛开的时节,通常指代重阳节。
⑤ 陶然:闲适愉悦的样子。

　　此时,白居易和刘禹锡(梦得)同在洛阳,白居易任太子少傅,是个闲职。二人饮酒闲谈,回首平生,难免有"早岁那知世事艰"的感慨。两人争着付钱买酒,相看都已67岁,虽有高雅情怀,却只能引经据史,行行酒令,听听知己的"清吟"奏出心灵的乐章而已。二人相约等到重阳佳节,家酿的菊花酒熟了,再到家里会饮,更能消愁解闷。全诗言简意富,语淡情长,见出炉火纯青的艺术功力。

Drinking Together with Liu Yuxi

While young, I was not worried about livelihood.
Now old, how could I grudge money for buying wine?
Let's spend ten thousand coins for a jarful of drink good!
Looking in face, two years more we'll be sixty-nine.
We read and play the drinkers' wager game at leisure;
Drunk, we listen to verse better than music light.
When chrysanthemums yellow, may I have the pleasure
To invite you to drink my home-brew with delight?

览卢子蒙侍御旧诗,多与微之唱和,感今伤昔,因赠子蒙,题于卷后

昔闻元九咏君诗,
恨与卢君相识迟。
今日逢君开旧卷,
卷中多道赠微之。
相看泪眼情难说,
别有伤心事岂知?
闻道①咸阳坟上树,
已抽三丈白杨枝。

① 闻道:听闻,听说。

白居易晚年与卢子蒙侍御交往,公元841年翻阅卢子蒙的旧诗集,发现不少诗是赠给元稹(元九,字微之)的,而元稹去世已经10年了。白居易不禁心酸,就写下了这首诗。头两句把30年前与元稹论诗衡文、谈笑风生的情景,重新展现在眼前。三、四句写今日与卢子蒙聚首,共同批阅他赠元稹的诗。五、六句写两个老人你望着我,我望着你,却都不说一句话。最后说,元稹坟上的白杨树枝都已三丈长了,树犹如此,人何以堪?这首七律悼念亡友,是一首情真意深的作品。

On Reading Lu Zimeng's Old Poems Written in the Same Rhyme Schemes as Yuan Zhen's Poems

I have read Yuan Zhen's verse on you of early date,
And I regret not to have known you till so late.
Today we read your verse together to the end,
I find so many poems on our deceased friend.
Looking at you in tears, what can I say at last?
Who else can know what broke my poor heart in the past?
I've heard say poplar trees in old capital loom
With branches thirty feet long over our friend's tomb.

红鹦鹉

安南远进红鹦鹉,

色似桃花语似人。

文章辩慧皆如此,

笼槛①何年出得身?

① 笼槛:囚困禽兽之处,此处指鸟笼。

　　这是白居易以议论入诗的一首七言绝句。第一句叙事,说红鹦鹉是远方进贡的珍禽。第二句状物,说明鹦鹉的色彩如花,言语似人。三、四句议论,说和红鹦鹉一样光彩夺目、能言善辩的知识分子,其实也和红鹦鹉一样被关在笼子里,什么时候才能飞出牢笼,恢复自由,一展宏图呢? 这首诗借物起兴,为天下不得志的读书人,吐出了一口不平的怨气。

The Red Cockatoo

Annam has sent us from afar a red cockatoo;

Colored like the peach blossom, it speaks as men do.

But it is shut up in a cage with bar on bar

Just as the learned or eloquent scholars are.

昼　卧

抱枕无言语,
空房独悄然①。　　　　　　　① 悄(qiǎo)然：形容寂静无声。
谁知尽日卧,
非病亦非眠。

　　这是白居易写孤寂心情的一首小诗。第一句写人,"抱枕"可见是独卧,"无言语"可见寂寞。第二句写境,"空房"更增加孤独之感,"悄然"更增加寂寞之情。第三句转为问话,"尽日卧"可见时间之长,"谁知"可见无人知晓,更加显得孤寂。第四句从反面作答,"非病"说明不是身体不好,"非眠"说明不是需要卧床；可见只是心情不佳,但又不便明说,而是有难言之隐。

Depression

Hugging my pillow, what to say?
My empty room's in silence deep.
Who knows I lie in bed all day,
Not ill and not even asleep?

病　中

交亲①不要苦相忧,　　　　　　　　① 交亲：亲戚朋友。
亦拟时时强出游。
但有心情何用脚?
陆乘肩舆②水乘舟。　　　　　　　　② 肩舆(yú)：即轿子。

　　这首七言绝句是作者答复友人探问病情的小诗。第一句不写友人慰问之情，反劝友人不必担忧，可见作者的乐天精神。第二句说明自己只要可能的话，还是时时想出去游玩的。第三句说明精神能够战胜物质困难，只要自己想走，并不一定需要步行。为什么呢？第四句答道：在陆地上可以坐轿，在水上可以乘船。这首小诗表现了作者的达观。

Illness

My bosom friends need not worry too much for me;
Somehow I'll take a walk if from illness I'm free.
When I want to go far, I need not use my feet;
Sedan by land and boat on water are as fleet.

杨柳枝词

一树春风千万枝,
嫩于金色软于丝。
永丰西角荒园里,
尽日无人属阿谁①?

① 阿(ā)谁:唐宋时期口语,即"谁",何人。

公元842年,白居易以刑部尚书退休后,寓居洛阳,有姬人樊素善歌,小蛮善舞,白居易写过诗句:"樱桃樊素口,杨柳小蛮腰。"这首词一说是为小蛮而写,一说只是写对人才埋没的感慨。第一句说春风吹拂,千丝万缕的柳枝随风起舞。第二句写柳枝绽出细叶嫩芽,望去一片嫩黄,比丝还要柔软。这两句把杨柳的生机横溢、秀色照人、轻盈袅娜,写得极为生动,有人认为是写小蛮舞姿之美。后两句一转,说杨柳长在永丰坊西角的荒园里,又有谁来一顾呢? 只好终日寂寞了。有人认为白居易担心身后小蛮的处境,颇有为浔阳江琵琶女一洒同情泪之感。

Song of Willow Branch

A tree of million branches sways in breeze of spring,
More tender and more soft than golden silk string by string.
In western corner of a garden in decay,
Who would come to admire its beauty all the day?

忆江南①

① 忆江南：本为唐代教坊曲名，后用作词牌名。

江南好，
风景旧曾谙②。
日出江花红胜火，
春来江水绿如蓝。
能不忆江南？

② 谙(ān)：熟悉。

公元 822—826 年，白居易先后任杭州、苏州刺史。回洛阳 12 年后 (838)，在 67 岁时，他写了三首《忆江南》词，这里选的是第一首。词一开头就说江南好，所以最后说不能不回忆。江南好并不是听人说，而是当年亲身感受到、体验过的。春来百花盛开，已极红艳，红日普照，更是红得耀眼；春江水绿，绿得胜过蓝草（蓝草叶子可制青绿染料）。由此可以看出白居易对大好河山的热爱。

Fair South Recalled

Fair Southern shore
With scenes I much adore,
At sunrise riverside flowers more red than fire,
In spring green river waves grow as blue as sapphire,
Which I can't but admire.

长 相 思[①]

[①] 长相思:词牌名,取自南朝乐府"上言长相思,下言久离别"一句,多写男女相思之情。

汴水流,
泗水流,
流到瓜洲古渡头。
吴山[②]点点愁。

[②] 吴山:位于今浙江省杭州市,春秋时期为吴国南界。

思悠悠,
恨悠悠,
恨到归时方始休。
月明人倚楼。

《长相思》是一首怀人念远的抒情小词,写妻子在月明之夜独自倚楼,望着汴水和泗水向南流去,想到远在江南的丈夫久久不归,就不免积相思为怨恨了。妻子可能是在徐州一带。唐代汴水由汴州(开封)流经徐州,与发源于山东的泗水汇合,转入运河,再向南流到扬州,在瓜

Everlasting Longing

See Northern river flow,
And Western river flow!
By Melon Islet, mingling waves, they go,
The Southern hills dotted with woe.

O how can I forget?
How can I not regret?
My deep sorrow will last till with you I have met,
Waiting from moonrise to moonset.

洲流入长江。瓜洲渡口在唐代是南北交通的要冲。面带点点愁容的吴山反映了妻子柔肠寸断的相思之情,这种相思无穷无尽,像悠悠不断的汴水和泗水一样,她一直从月出等到月落,要等到丈夫回家才能罢休。

图书在版编目（CIP）数据

许渊冲译白居易诗选：许渊冲英译作品：汉英对照 /（唐）白居易著；许渊冲编译 . -- 北京：中译出版社，2021.1（2022.7 重印）

ISBN 978-7-5001-6453-1

Ⅰ. ①许… Ⅱ. ①白… ②许… Ⅲ. ①唐诗－诗集－汉、英 Ⅳ. ①I222.742

中国版本图书馆CIP数据核字（2020）第 240380 号

出版发行	中译出版社
地　　址	北京市西城区新街口外大街28号普天德胜大厦主楼4层
电　　话	(010) 68359719
邮　　编	100088
电子邮箱	book@ctph.com.cn
网　　址	http://www.ctph.com.cn
出版人	乔卫兵
总策划	刘永淳
责任编辑	刘香玲　张　旭
文字编辑	王秋璎　张莞嘉　赵浠彤
营销编辑	毕竞方
赏　　析	李　旻
封面制作	刘　哲
内文制作	黄　浩　北京竹页文化传媒有限公司
印　　刷	天津新华印务有限公司
经　　销	新华书店
规　　格	840mm×1092mm　1/32
印　　张	4.75
字　　数	100千
版　　次	2021年1月第1版
印　　次	2022年7月第3次

ISBN 978-7-5001-6453-1　定价：39.00元

版权所有　侵权必究

中译出版社